WELCOME TO THE WORLD
OF
Geronimo Stilton

Published by Sweet Cherry Publishing Limited
Unit 36, Vulcan House,
Vulcan Road,
Leicester, LE5 3EF
United Kingdom

First published in the UK in 2020
2020 edition

2 4 6 8 10 9 7 5 3 1

ISBN: 978-1-78226-532-0

Text by Geronimo Stilton
Art Director: Iacopo Bruno
Graphic Designer: Andrea Cavallini / theWorldofDOT
Original cover illustration by Andrea Da Rold (design) and Andrea Cavallini (colour)
Concept of illustration by Larry Keys,
produced by Claudio Cernuschi (design) and Cristina Giorgilli (colour)
Initial and final page illustrations by Roberto Ronchi and Ennio Bufi, MAD5 (design) and Studio
Parlapà and Andrea Cavallini (colour). Map illustrations by Andrea Da Rold and Andrea Cavallini
Cover layout and typography by Margot Reverdiau
Interior layout and typography by Margot Reverdiau
Graphics by Merenguita Gingermouse and Gherardo di Lenna
© 2001-2015 Edizioni Piemme S.p.A., Palazzo Mondadori – Via Mondadori, 1 – 20090 Segrate
© 2020 UK edition, Sweet Cherry Publishing
International Rights © Atlantyca S.p.A. – via Leopardi 8, 20123 Milano, Italy
Translation © 2005 by Atlantyca S.p.A.

Original title: *Attenti Ai Baffi... Arriva Topigoni!*
Based on an original idea by Elisabetta Dami

www.geronimostilton.com/uk

Stilton is the name of a famous English cheese. It is a registered trademark of the Stilton Cheese Makers'
Association. For more information go to www.stiltoncheese.com

Not to be sold outside the UK

www.sweetcherrypublishing.com

Printed and bound in Turkey
T.IO006

Geronimo Stilton

THE MYSTERY OF THE ROARING RAT

Sweet Cherry

THE ROARING RAT

It was a sunny July morning. The sun was so **HOT**, you could grill a cheese sandwich on the path.

I went to have breakfast at the corner café (as usual). I ordered a coffee and a **CHEESE DANISH PASTRY** (as usual). Then I went to the newsstand (as usual). I wanted to get a freshly printed copy of my newspaper …

... Oh, but I haven't told you yet. My name is Stilton, *Geronimo Stilton*. I run The Rodent's Gazette. It's the most popular newspaper here on Mouse Island.

As I was saying, I went to get a copy of my newspaper (as usual). But something *unusual* was going on. I could not find a copy of the paper. Not a single one!

I was so puzzled, I had to ask the newsagent about it. "Excuse me, **INKYPAWS**," I said. "I am looking for my usual copy of The Rodent's Gazette."

INKYPAWS looked uncomfortable. He scratched his whiskers. "Err ... umm ... I don't have one!" he said.

Now I was even more puzzled. "Why not? Are you sold out?"

INKYPAWS shook his head. He stared at his paws. "Mr. Stilton, the truth is ... I do not sell The Rodent's Gazette anymore!" he blurted out.

I couldn't believe my big mouse ears. "Since when?"

INKYPAWS pointed to the piles of newspapers. They all had the same title at the top – *The Roaring Rat!*

"A one-eyed rat came by this morning," he

explained. "He offered me an enormouse amount of money to sell nothing but *The Roaring Rat.* Then he took away all the copies of The Rodent's Gazette."

I stared at **INKYPAWS**, unable to squeak.

"I'm sorry, Mr. Stilton," **INKYPAWS** said. "Business is business!" He waved a **CHEQUE** in front of my snout. It was from *The Roaring Rat*. And it had more zeroes than a hunk of Swiss cheese has holes.

"That **STINKS** worse than a mound of mouldy

cheese!" I fumed. I grabbed a copy of *The Roaring Rat*. I wanted to see what this one-eyed rat was up to.

As I read the front-page story, my whiskers started to twitch.

The Roaring Rat

STILTON'S PAPER IS ON THE WAY OUT

The Rodent's Gazette is going broke! *The Roaring Rat* has learned that newsstands will no longer sell the newspaper. Bookstores will not sell books by Stilton Publishing. Keep reading *The Roaring Rat* to get the whole story. You won't miss *The Rodent's Gazette* – we promise!

A One-Eyed Rat

I **hurried** to the office as fast as my paws could take me. I had to find out what was going on!

On the way, I passed a bookstore. I looked in the window (as usual). There is always a copy of my latest book displayed there.

But this was not a usual morning. My latest book was not in the window. I ran inside. I searched high and low, but I could not find a single book by my company, Stilton Publishing. Instead, all of the books came from a new company – The Roaring Rat Group!

Batsabout Books, the owner of the store, looked nervous to see me. *Batsabout* is a little snobby, but he has always been happy to sell my books.

"I take it you've heard the news, Mr. Stilton," he squeaked. "I'm sorry, but I can no longer sell books from Stilton Publishing. I received a proposal from a one-eyed rat early this morning …"

Batsabout showed me a **CHEQUE** from The Roaring Rat Group. This one had so many zeroes it made me dizzy. I turned as pale as a piece of mozzarella. Then I left the store without a word.

"This is much worse than I thought," I muttered. I hurried to 17 Swiss Cheese Centre. My whiskers were trembling. I rushed into my office. Then I screamed for my secretary. **"Mousellllaaaaaaaa!"**

???
WHO IS THIS MYSTERIOUS RAT?

The entire staff of my newspaper came running into my office. They were all squeaking at once.

"Mr. Stilton? Did you hear the news?"

"Every newsstand on the island is carrying only *The Roaring Rat*!"

"Every bookstore is selling only books by The Roaring Rat Group!"

I sank into my chair. "This means things are much, much worse than I thought!" I cried.

I needed more information. I turned on the television. Walter Newsynose, the famous reporter on New Mouse Island, was giving a **special edition** report.

"We have **breaking news**," Walter said. "This morning, a mysterious one-eyed rat went to every

newsstand and bookstore on Mouse Island. The rat
claimed to be the owner of The Roaring Rat Group.
He bought every book and paper by Stilton Publishing
and had them sent to the recycling centre. Who is this
mysterious rat who is ruining Geronimo Stilton?"

My whiskers quivered. My tail trembled. I jumped
out of my seat.

"PUTRID CHEESE PUFFS!" I yelled. **"This is
much, much, *much* worse than I thought!"**

William Shortpaws, Also Known as Cheap Mouse Willy

At that moment, the phone **RANG**. I answered it.

"Hello. Is this Stilton, *Geronimo Stilton*?"

It was Aunt Sweetfur, my favourite auntie. When I was a little mouselet, she read bedtime stories to me: 'Jack and the Cheese Stick', 'Snow Rat and the Seven Mice', 'Little Red Ratty Hood' – all of the greats.

"Nephew, I have some bad news for you," Aunt Sweetfur began. "Dreadful news. I don't know how to put this. It's about Grandfather William."

A shiver ran through my fur. Everyone is afraid of my grandfather William Shortpaws, also known as **Cheap Mouse Willy**. He is the founder of The

Rodent's Gazette. He thinks nobody knows how to run a newspaper but him.

"Aunt Sweetfur, tell me the truth," I said. "Is Grandfather William ill?"

A loud voice roared on the other end of the phone. "Fat chance!" It was Grandfather William! "I'm feeling fine, Grandson. But you had better do something right now to save the company! If you don't, I am coming back to take over Stilton Publishing. **IS THAT CLEAR?**"

How was I supposed to save the company from a mysterious one-eyed rat? I started to protest. "But Grandfather—"

"Stop squeaking and get moving!" Grandfather William yelled. Then he hung up on me.

17

I felt pretty **TERRIBLE**. This was worse than the time I got cheddar chewing gum stuck in my whiskers. Worse than that time I had the mousles and broke out in red spots all over my **FUR**. Worse than when I had a bad reaction to some overripe Muenster and thought I was allergic to cheese.

I started to sob. Soon my snout was **SOAKED** with tears. **"This means things are much, much, much, *much* worse than I thought!"**

THAT'S HITTING BELOW THE BELT!

The phone rang again. This time it was LEONA MISERMOUSE. She is the owner of 17 Swiss Cheese Centre. She is very rich, but she hates to spend any money. She reminds me of Grandfather William.

"Good morning, Mr. Stilton," LEONA began. She sounded nervous. "I'm afraid I must ask you to leave the building. This morning a one-eyed rat offered me an **ENORMOUSE** amount of money to rent your offices. Of course, I said yes."

I felt like I had been hit by a cheese truck. "**WHAT?** Are you kicking us out of the building?"

"I'm ever so sorry," said LEONA. But she didn't sound sorry. "I would like you to leave as soon as possible. The new owner's furniture will be there this afternoon."

"This afternoon!" I squeaked louder than a mouse whose tail has been run over by a cheese delivery truck. "This is **outrageous!**"

My anger did not seem to bother LEONA MISERMOUSE. "Business is business, Mr. Stilton," she said. "The owner of *The Roaring Rat* offered me so much money, I couldn't say no."

I hung up the phone. I fell back into my chair. I thumped my snout on my desk.

"Things are much, much, much, much, *much* worse than I thought!" I moaned.

HE SHOULD BE
ASHAMED OF HIMSELF!

The phone rang again. I picked it up. **"What now?"** I squeaked. I just knew it had to be more bad news.

I was right. On the other end was **LEDGER MONEYMOUSE**. He is the manager of Ratlay's Bank. The Rodent's Gazette borrows a lot of money from Ratlay's.

I knew what was coming. "I bet you are going to tell me that you are calling in all of our loans," I said.

MONEYMOUSE squeaked "YES!"

I kept going. "And I bet you're going to tell me you're sorry, but we can't borrow money from you anymore."

"YES! YES!"

I went on. "And I bet you're going to tell me that Ratlay's Bank was just bought by a one-eyed rat."

"YES! YES! YES!" Moneymouse shouted.

I shouted right back at him. "Tell him he is not playing fair! He should be **ashamed** of himself, whoever he is!"

I slammed down the phone. My whiskers were drooping. My paws were shaking.

"This means things are much, much, much, much, much, *much* worse than I thought!" I wailed.

WE ARE IN BIG TROUBLE!

I couldn't take the stress anymore. Things were moving fast. **TOO FAST**. Faster than a hamster on a treadmill. Faster than being chased by a cat. Faster than New Mouse City's annual rat race!

I fainted. Mousella took a piece of blue cheese and waved it under my nose. The strong smell woke me up. I could hear my staff members muttering.

"Who is this mysterious one-eyed rat?"

"Why does he want to ruin *The Rodent's Gazette*?"

I came to my senses. What kind of a mouse was I? My staff needed me. I had to be strong!

"QUIET!" I shouted. Everyone stared at me.

"It's true. We are in **big** trouble," I said. "But that just means we have to be strong. We have to stay calm. There is a solution for every problem. We will get through this!"

Everyone cheered. Then DUSTY DUSTWELL, the cleaning lady, spoke up. "Great speech, Mr. Stilton. So what do we do now?"

I smoothed my fur. I wiggled my ears. I cleared my throat. I opened my mouth to speak ... and burst into tears!

"**I DON'T KNOOOOOOOOOOOOOOOOOOOW!!!**" I wailed.

I fell to the floor, crying. Through my sobs, I could hear the other mice talking about me.

"Poor Mr. Stilton!"

"After all he has done for the company."

"What will **Cheap Mouse Willy** have to say about this?"

"I am sure he will do something terrible to Geronimo!"

"This is worse than a hunk of Swiss cheese with no holes!"

"Worse than being caught in a rat trap!"

"Worse than a cheeseburger with no cheese!"

"Slimy Swiss rolls, I'm glad I'm not in Mr. Stilton's fur right now!"

MOUSE TEARS

The door to my office flew open. My sister, Thea, burst into the room. She is the special correspondent for The Rodent's Gazette. She held my favourite nephew, Benjamin, by the paw.

"**Gerry Berry**!" she yelled. "Dry those tears! This is no time for SNIVELLING! You must do something! Now!"

Benjamin ran up to me. He **kissed** the tip of my snout. "Yes, Uncle Geronimo. You must do something before it's too late!"

I squeezed my **TEAR-SOAKED** pawkerchief. A salty puddle had formed at my feet. "But what can I do?" I sobbed.

Thea scolded me. "Shame on you, Geronimo. Snap out of it! You can't let the company go down without a fight!"

Thea was right. I wiped my whiskers. Then I turned to my staff.

"Friends," I began, choking back tears. "We have known one another for a long time. We have shared good times and bad times here at The Rodent's Gazette. We are a team. Today, I need my team more than ever. Can I count on your help?"

The staff were silent for a moment. Then they all shouted, "YESSSSSSSSSSSS!"

I knew this was an important moment. I had the staff behind me. We had to do something. It was now or never.

I glanced at a copy of The Rodent's Gazette from the day before. The page was open to the classifieds. Out of the corner of my eye, I noticed an ad:

The ad gave me an idea. I grabbed the paper. Then I waved it in the air like a flag.

"If we can't sell our products in bookstores and newsstands, we will find some other way to sell them!" I announced. "And I know just the mouse for the job. Our old business manager, Shif T. Paws! I swear on my collection of antique cheese rinds, we will pull through this! Three cheers for The Rodent's Gazette!"

The staff let out a shout. "**Hurrah! Hurrah! Hurrah!** Hurrah for Geronimo Stilton! Hurrah for The Rodent's Gazette!"

WHEN YOU GET RIGHT DOWN TO IT ...

I called the number in the ad and left a message. Then I waited.

I didn't have to wait long. Five minutes later, I heard a voice outside my door.

"Watch your whiskers. Here comes Shif T. Paws!

S is for **Super salesmouse!**

H is for **Happy times ahead!**

I is for **Improving your business!**

F is for **Fast results!**

T is for **Time to get moving!**

P is for **Put your paws together!**

A is for **All is not lost!**

W is for **Watch your whiskers!**

S is for **Stop your worrying!**

Shif T. Paws is here!"

The door flew open. It slammed into my snout, **CRUSHING** my whiskers. I stuck to the door like cheese on pizza. Then I slid to the floor and fainted.

Mousella revived me with more blue cheese. I opened my eyes and saw the mouse who had flung the door open.

He was a tall rodent wearing a grey suit and striped tie. The top of his head was as round and furless as a ball of mozzarella. Wire-rimmed **GLASSES** perched on the tip of his snout. Mobile phones hung all over him like ornaments on a Christmas tree. He had a yellow mobile phone behind his right ear, a red mobile phone in the pocket of his jacket, a blue one in his shirt pocket, a green one in his back trouser pocket, and a pink mobile phone hung around his neck.

"Shif!" I cried, bouncing up to my paws. "It's **GREAT** to see you again."

You see, Shif T. had worked at The Rodent's Gazette before. In fact, he'd helped me out of a tough spot when

my grandfather, William Shortpaws (also known as **Cheap Mouse Willy**), had **fired** the entire staff.

Shif T. had left us a year ago to pursue a business opportunity in **RATZIKISTAN**, selling **ICE** to Eskimice. Only a salesmouse like Shif T. could pull something like that off. I had no idea he'd come back to New Mouse City, but **HOLEY CHEESE**, was I glad he had!

"Good morning, Mr. Stilton. It's great to be back," he replied in a loud voice. "You called the right mouse!"

I stepped back, startled. "There is no need to shout," I said. "My ears are not stuffed with cheese!"

But Shif T. only got louder. "When you get right down to it, Stilton, **how big is the company these days?**" he asked.

I started to reply. "Well, we have about—"

He did not wait for me to finish. "When you get right down to it, **what is the problem?**"

I tried again. "Well, the problem is—"

"When you get right down to it, **what is my salary?**"

I wasn't sure what to say. "I think—"

"When you get right down to it, double your offer and I can start right now. **Where's my office?** Ah, that way … I guessed as much. I'll be right back!"

Before I could think, Shif T. grabbed the blue cheese from Mousella.

"Blue cheese! My **favourite!**" he squeaked. Then he turned and ran out of my office. I heard him yell as he scurried down the hall. "Watch your whiskers, here

comes Shif T. Paws! I'm running the show here now! Move your tails, everyone! It's selling time!"

"That Shif T. Paws is a born salesmouse," Mousella whispered. "You are lucky to have him, Mr. Stilton."

"Do you think so?" I asked. **I really wasn't sure!**

COME ON, IT'S SELLING TIME!

Thirty seconds later, the door flew open again.

I jumped.

Shif T. Paws was back! He hopped on my desk. He took a microphone out of his jacket. Then he began to squeak orders at my staff.

"We need to sell. Sell, sell, sell. S-E-L-L! Get it?" he shouted. "SEEEEEEEEEEEEEELLL!"

He paused. Then he announced his plan.

FIRST TARGET:
Supermarkets and shopping centres!
We will stand at all the entrances and sell newspapers to the rodents while they shop!

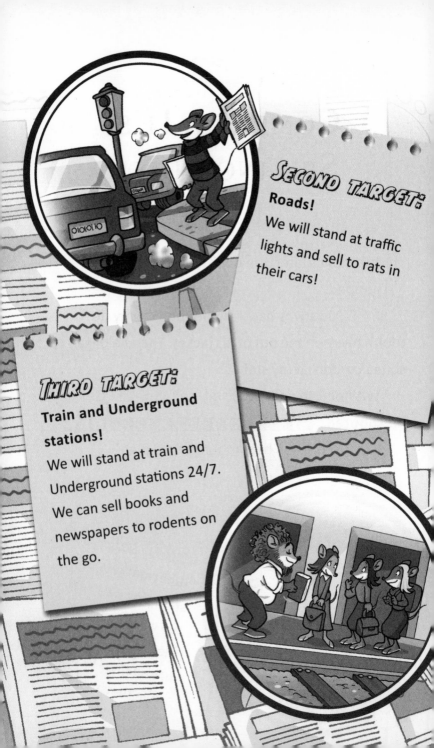

SECOND TARGET:
Roads!
We will stand at traffic lights and sell to rats in their cars!

THIRD TARGET:
Train and Underground stations!
We will stand at train and Underground stations 24/7. We can sell books and newspapers to rodents on the go.

FOURTH TARGET:

Door-to-door!
We will knock on the door of every house and apartment in New Mouse City with hot-off-the-press copies of The Rodent's Gazette.

FIFTH TARGET:

Beaches!
Rodents getting their fur tanned need to read, too! We will go to all of the beaches on Mouse Island to sell our books and newspapers!

SIXTH TARGET:

Cinemas!
We will sell to rodents as they come and go to the cinema!

Shif T.'s eyes **shone** behind his glasses. **"Are you all with me? Come on, it's selling time!"** he yelled.

The staff were silent for a moment. They all looked at one another.

Then they cried out, "**Hurrah** for Shif T. Paws!"

"That's the spirit!" Shif T. shouted. "We will save The Rodent's Gazette!"

Everyone cheered. Then Shif T. suddenly looked upset.

"CRUSTY KEYPADS!" Shif T. shrieked. "I've lost my favourite mobile phone!"

The salesmouse ran out of the room. I stepped forwards. I wanted to inspire my staff the way Shif T. Paws had.

"Friends—" I began.

But a cry rang out: "Watch your whiskers, Shif T. Paws is here!"

Shif T. ran back into the office, pushing open the door. Once again, it

slammed into me. I was as flat as a slice of American cheese. I slid to the floor.

"Good news, Stilton," Shif T. said. "I found my mobile phone. I left it in the bathroom."

Luckily, Mousella had another piece of blue cheese. The smell worked instantly. I stood up.

Shif T. Paws gave the microphone to **Kreamy O'Cheddar**. She is the editor-in-chief of the newspaper. She is also a good friend.

"I would like to make an announcement," she said. "The staff of *The Rodent's Gazette* will give up their holiday time so we can work to save the newspaper."

I was so moved! I secretly wiped a tear from my eye.

Kreamy went on. "We have also agreed to work for free until these tough times are over."

Shif T. Paws slapped me on the back. "We will pull through, Stilton," he said. "When you get right down to it, **we will save the paper**. I'll stake my fur on it – **or my name isn't Shif T. Paws**!"

MY FUR FELT FRIED!

Shif T. Paws took back the microphone. "We need to find new offices right away. Any ideas?"

Mousella spoke up. "My cousin is a baker," she said. "His name is **Bagel Buckwheat**. He has a large basement at 85 Curds Court. We could move the business there for now."

"Excellent!" Shif T. said. "We will all meet at eleven o'clock tonight at 85 Curds Court. Now, everyone come and take a pile of books and papers. Move those tails! It's selling time!"

Bagel Buckwheat

Everyone took their piles and headed out to enact Shif T.'s plan. Everyone but Thea, that is. She was sitting at the computer, surfing the Internet. I could tell by the look on her face that she had an IDEA.

Before I could ask her about it, Shif T. hung a sack of newspapers around my shoulders. Then he stuffed a **huge pile** of books into my paws.

"Move your tail, Stilton!" he squeaked. "We need to sell every last copy before tonight! It's selling time!"

I started to protest. "But–"

Shif T. Paws pushed me out the door. "See you at eleven, Stilton!"

I left the building, shaking my head. It was hard to argue with Shif T. Paws.

I found a good selling spot at the corner of Limburger Lane and Parmesan Place. I stood right next to the traffic light. When drivers stopped at the red light, I would shout, "Papers! Get the latest news fresh off the press!"

CHEESE NIBLETS, I had a tough time! It was so

hot that all of the drivers had their air conditioners on and their windows shut. Most of them pretended not to see me.

I tried pushing the books. "Books for sale! Nothing beats a good book on a hot summer day!"

But only a few people stopped to buy anything.

The day dragged on. It got hotter and hotter. My fur felt **FRIED**. And I had forgotten to put sunscreen on my snout!

I felt like giving up. I was about to walk away when a long, fancy car pulled up. Riding in the back were several female mice. I recognised one of them – the snobby MRS. EDWARD S. SMUGRAT III.

I heard Mrs. Smugrat whisper, "Isn't that Stilton, *Geronimo Stilton*?"

"Oh, it's him all right!" one of her friends replied. "I hear he is ruined! It all happened in one morning! Can you believe it?"

Mrs. Smugrat handed a large coin to her driver and whispered something. He rolled down the window, examined me ^{UP} and _{DOWN,} then gave the money to me.

"Give me a copy of the newspaper," he said. "And keep the change!"

I blushed with embarrassment.

But then I realised I shouldn't be embarrassed. I was just trying to save my newspaper, *BY CHEDDAR!*

I straightened my tail and took the coin. That's one more copy sold, I thought.

I felt better after that. I decided to keep going. **"Papers! Papers! Get the latest news fresh off the press!"**

LIFE IS BEAUTIFUL

By the time evening fell, my snout was sunburned. My paws were covered with blisters from standing all day. My spirits were **low**. And I was as hungry as a jumbo-size **CAT**. All I wanted to do was go home and curl up with a cream cheese smoothie. But Shif T. Paws had called that eleven o'clock meeting. I couldn't let down my staff. So I dragged myself to 85 Curds Court. I saw the baker's sign on the building:

BUCKWHEAT'S BAKERY
THE BEST BREAD
YOU'LL EVER BUY!

I walked inside and found myself in a basement. The smell of freshly baked bread filled my snout.

A small rodent with twinkling eyes came towards me. He shook my paw.

"Hi there, Boss," he said in a friendly voice. "I'm Bagel Buckwheat. I hear business isn't so good."

"My name is Stilton, *Geronimo Stilton*," I said. "I'm very grateful for your help. We are going through a tough time. But I'm sure we'll pull through."

Bagel **SLAPPED** me on the shoulder. He left a white flour pawprint on my sleeve.

"Of course you'll pull through, **BOSS**!" he said cheerfully. "Never give up, that's what I always say. keep hanging on and things will work out. You can stay here as long as you need. Which reminds me. I'm not rich, but if you ever need a small loan …"

I shook my head, touched. What a nice mouse!

Bagel gave me a closer look and frowned. "Boss, you're looking a little pale. Have you eaten today?"

Before I could answer, he pulled out a tray from one of the ovens. Then he handed me a piece of French bread covered with melted cheese.

"Have a good munch, and life will look a lot better," Bagel said. "My cheese bread is guaranteed to bring a smile to your snout!"

"Thank you," I said. "You are very kind."

"No need to thank me," Bagel said. "I'm happy to help. Now, eat up while the bread is still **HOT**!"

I took a bite and licked my whiskers. **That cheese bread was delicious!**

I'M TOO FOND OF MY TAIL

The whole staff arrived for the meeting. We gathered around a pile of flour sacks. Bagel handed out cheese bread to everyone.

Shif T. Paws was standing on a sack, adding up the day's sales.

"Nifty!" he squeaked. "You all did well." Then he jumped down. "We need a **BIG** pile of cash to get the publishing house back on its paws. But don't worry. *I HAVE AN IDEA.*"

Shif T. slapped me on the shoulders. "Now it's your turn, Stilton!"

"What do you mean, my turn?" I asked, puzzled.

He winked at me. "Stilton, do you know the television game show called **THE MOUSETRAP**?"

I nodded. **THE MOUSETRAP** is a game show with a spooky theme. I try not to watch it. I'm a bit of a 'fraidy mouse, you see, and spooky things give me nightmares!

"Well, then you know it takes place at midnight," Shif T. continued. "The player sits in a mousetrap. When he or she gives the wrong answer, the trap pinches his or her tail – sometimes even **CHOPS iT OFF**! Right then and there, on live TV!"

I shuddered. "What does this have to do with me?"

Shif T. smiled widely. "Because YOU are the next contestant, Stilton!"

"**PUTRID CHEESE PUFFS!**" I shrieked. "No way! Never! I'm too fond of my tail!"

I tried to flee, but Shif T. grabbed my tail. "Now, Stilton, don't disappoint me," he said. "You asked me to save this publishing company and I will. But I can't do it alone. I'm just asking for a small favour."

I stamped my paw. "Small favour? This is a **BIG** deal! I could lose my tail!"

"Or you could win a million pounds," Shif T. pointed out.

I paused. A **MILLION POUNDS** would solve all of our problems. We desperately needed that money.

"BUT WHY DOES IT HAVE TO BE MEEEE?" I wailed nervously.

Mousella stepped up. "Nobody here is as smart as you are, Mr. Stilton. You know a little something about everything! If anyone can win on THE MOUSETRAP, it's you!"

I sighed. I hated to admit it, but Mousella was right. I am a brainy mouse.

"Now things are much, much, much, much, much, much, *much* worse than I thought!" I cried. "But I have no choice. I'll do it. I'll do it for The Rodent's Gazette!"

Shif T. Paws let out a cheer. "Well done, Stilton. We'll make a million! By the way, you are going on tonight's show. Are you ready? Are you?"

But I didn't hear him. I had fainted again.

It's a good thing Mousella always has blue cheese nearby!

THE MOUSETRAP

Who can blame me for fainting again? **THE MOUSETRAP** is very dangerous. Besides, I'm a very shy mouse. The idea of going on a live game show, in front of millions of rodents, made my fur stand on end.

Bagel gave me another piece of **HOT** cheese bread to cheer me up. He tucked a third into my jacket pocket. "You never know," he said. "You may get hungry later."

But I didn't feel like eating. My tummy was doing flip-flops. Shif T. Paws dragged me out of the bakery and drove me to the television studio. I think he was afraid I would try to run away at the last minute. **I hate to say it, but he was right!**

We pulled up in front of the Top TV studios. It was almost midnight, and stars shone in the night sky.

We stepped out of the car, and an assistant came to greet us.

"Which one of you is the contestant?" he asked.

"Uh ... I am," I said nervously.

He shook my paw. "It's an honour to meet you. You must be a very brave mouse to appear on a dangerous game show like **THE MOUSETRAP**!"

I did not feel like a very brave mouse. My tail trembled as the assistant led us into the studio. He took us to the host of the show, VLAD TORTURETAIL. He was a pale mouse with pointed teeth. He wore a black suit, a white silk shirt, and a red

VLAD TORTURETAIL

58

cape over his shoulders. He looked like a **vampire rat!**

TORTURETAIL looked me over. "So, are you tonight's VICtIM – I mean, contestant?" he asked in a creepy voice. **"I hope you are not too fond of your tail. Heh, heh, heh."**

I turned pale. I tried to sneak towards the exit, but Shif T. Paws pulled me back.

"Stilton, don't give up now!" he said. "Think of your company! Think of your staff!"

"All I can think about is my poor tail!" I wailed.

Shif T. lowered his voice. "Come on, Stilton. What's more important? Your tail or The Rodent's Gazette?"

"Good question," I replied. "Let me go think about that and I'll get back to you."

I tried to slip away again, but this time

TORTURETAIL grabbed me. By the tail!

"You can't escape," he hissed. "The studio doors are locked. The trap is ready!"

I gulped.

"Twenty seconds to go, Stilton," TORTURETAIL cackled. "Keep your cool, or you'll lose your tail!" Then he laughed that creepy laugh of his again. **"Heh, heh, heh, heh, heh!"**

GOOD LUCK, STILTON!

Suddenly, the lights in the studio went out. A big clock began striking the hours.

ONE … **TWO** … **THREE** … **FOUR** … **FIVE** … **SIX** … **SEVEN** … **EIGHT** … **NINE** … **TEN** … **ELEVEN** … **TWELVE** … twelve strokes. It was midnight!

The lights came back on. I blinked. Two sturdy rats grabbed me.

"Your hour has come, Stilton!" they growled.

They dragged me toward a huge mousetrap. It looked like every rodent's worst nightmare. But I didn't try to fight them. It was too late to turn back now!

Behind me, Shif T. Paws called out, "Good luck, Stilton!"

"I'll need it," I squeaked weakly.

Stay calm, Geronimo, I told myself. *Do it for* The Rodent's Gazette*!*

The rats slipped my tail under the spring in the trap. They put my paws in chains. Now it was **DEFINITELY** too late to turn back!

Vlad TORTURETAIL came out holding a microphone. "Meet tonight's VICTIM – I mean, contestant – Mr. Geronimo Stilton from New Mouse City!"

C. E. Metery

S. Pectre

G. Host

M. Ummy

G. Rave

C. Rypt

T. Ombstone

F. Rankenstein

V. Ampire

MIND YOUR TAIL, STILTON!

I studied the members of the game show jury. They had such strange names and spooky snouts!

TORTURETAIL glared at me. "Tell us, Mr. Stilton. What do you do for a living?"

C. ORPSE
C. OFFIN
M. ONSTER
G. H. OUL
S. CARY

C. REEPY
D. RACULA
S. H. IVER
B. ONES
H. OWL

I cleared my throat. "Er, I am a publisher and an author. I run the most popular newspaper in New Mouse City, The Rodent's Gazette."

The game show host snickered. "I have heard that business is not so good lately, Mr. Stilton," he said. "Is that why you are playing our little game? Are you that desperate for money? HEH, HEH, HEH."

I blushed. What kind of a question was that? I looked at Shif T. Paws. He gave me two thumbs up and mouthed the words **ONE MILLION POUNDS**.

I felt a little more confident. "The reason I am playing this game is strictly personal," I answered. "I prefer to keep it to myself, if you don't mind."

TORTURETAIL snarled. He was disappointed that he hadn't rattled me. "Of course,"

he said. "Let's move on to the questions. You know by now that a wrong answer will release the spring on the mousetrap. When the trap falls, it will pinch your tail – or even **CHOP iT OFF!**"

I shuddered. My whiskers were quivering uncontrollably.

The audience just laughed.

A big, stocky rat with coal-black fur and very muscular arms began to pound a drum.

DUM … 　DUM … 　DUM … 　DUM …

I could feel the excitement in the room begin to rise. The audience were on the edge of their seats. I looked into the control room and saw the director rubbing his paws with glee. I realised that the ratings were probably going up! Every rodent on Mouse Island was probably tuned in to see me **LOSE MY TAIL**.

"Here comes the first question," TORTURETAIL howled. **"Mind your tail, Stilton! Heh, heh, heh, heh, heh!"**

ARE YOU SURE YOU'RE READY, MR. STILTON?

"Are you ready, Mr. Stilton?" TORTURETAIL asked.

I took a deep breath. "Yes," I said. "I'm ready."

"Are you **sure** you're ready, Mr. Stilton?" TORTURETAIL asked again.

"Yes, thank you," I said again. "I'm ready."

Him: "Ready, ready, *ready*?"

Me: "Yes, very ready."

Him: "Are you sure?"

Me: "Yes, I'm sure!"

Him: "Are you very, *very* sure?"

Me: "I said **I'M SURE!**"

Him: "Can I start with the first question?"

Me: "**YES!**"

Him: "You know, you still don't look ready to me ..."

Me: "**I AM READY!**"

Him: "You're looking a little pale ..."

Me: "I am **NOT** pale!"

Him: "I see some sweat on your whiskers. You seem upset."

I couldn't take any more of this. "Please, please, *please* ask the question!" I begged.

TORTURETAIL seemed pleased. He had stressed me out – which was his plan all along, of course.

"The first question is **REALLY** easy, Mr. Stilton," he said. "But only if you know the answer! Heh, heh, heh."

The members of the jury laughed meanly. I wiped the sweat off my whiskers and tried to relax.

"First question," TORTURETAIL said in a serious voice. "Can you tell us the original meaning of the word ... Halloween?"

The black rat began to beat the drum again.

DUM ...   DUM ...   DUM ...

This was an easy question for me! I had recently published a book called *It's Halloween, You 'Fraidy Mouse!* that included a brief history of Halloween.

So I cleared my throat. "Actually, yes, I can tell you. Halloween is an old Celtic word. The Celts from Northern Europe were the first to celebrate Halloween. They danced around fires wearing masks."

Halloween?

I paused dramatically. "Therefore, the word Halloween comes from **All Hallows' Eve**!"

"Is that your FINAL answer?" TORTURETAIL asked me. His beady eyes seemed to pierce through my fur.

"Yes," I said confidently.

"Are you **SURE**?" he asked again in a menacing voice.

"I am quite sure," I said.

TORTURETAIL seemed disappointed. He shook his head. "The answer is ... CORRECT!"

The jury began to jeer. "BOOOOOO!"

I realised they were disappointed too. They wanted to see blood. *My* blood!

TORTURETAIL asked the second question. "What is the name of the substance used by the Ancient Egyptians to preserve dead bodies? It also gave us the word 'mummy'."

At first, I thought my tail was **LOST**. I could not think of the answer. The drum boomed in the background.

MVMMY

DUM ...   DUM ...   DUM ...

Then I remembered an adventure I had in Egypt. I wrote about it in *The Curse of the Cheese Pyramid*. I smiled.

"I am sure the name is 'mum'," I said. "It was a sticky mixture of bitumen, myrrh and other substances used to preserve dead bodies."

TORTURETAIL scowled. "CORRECT!" he howled.

The jury jeered again. "**BOOOOO!**"

70

Offstage, Shif T. Paws shot me a big grin. Things were going well. I still had my tail. And it hadn't even been pinched yet!

"Third question!" **TORTURETAIL** shrieked. "What is the name of the legendary king who led the Knights of the Rat Table?"

This one was *very* easy. My aunt **Sweetfur** read me stories of the knights when

KING RATTHUR

I was just a wee mouselet. "King Ratthur!" I replied.

TORTURETAIL scowled. "Correct again!"

The jury **BOOED** me once more. Then they began to mutter among themselves.

"These questions are much too easy!"

"They promised us blood, but so far they haven't even pinched his tail!"

"That Stilton is as sharp as a block of cheddar!"

I smiled under my whiskers. **TORTURETAIL**

DRACULA

looked miserable. He read the fourth question.

"What is the name of the Irish writer who wrote the famous book *Dracula* in 1897?"

"Bram Mouser!" I answered immediately.

TORTURETAIL mumbled under his whiskers. "Correct."

BOOOOOOO! the jury shouted.

TORTURETAIL cleared his throat. "The last question is worth ONE MILLION POUNDS," he said. "No rodent has ever answered the final question correctly before. It has five parts:

1. Who wrote the novel *Rattenstein*?

2. When was the author born and when did the author die?

3. When was the novel written and why?

4. What is the name of the mad scientist who creates the monster?

72

5. Where does the action take place?
You have one minute to give your answer, Mr. Stilton!"

I closed my eyes and tried to concentrate. This question was harder than a block of stale cheddar! The drum pounded in my ears.

DUM ...   DUM ...   DUM ...

As the head of a publishing company, I know a lot about books. But if I made even one mistake, I could bid my tail bye-bye!

"We're **WAITING**, Stilton," **TORTURETAIL** hissed.

It was now or never. I shouted out the answers.

"**1.** The novel *Rattenstein* was written by Ratty Wollstonecraft Shelley!

2. She was born in 1797 and died in 1851!

3. Shelley began writing the novel in 1816. She was at a party with friends and everyone was telling scary stories. This gave her the idea for a monster created by a mad scientist!

73

RATTENSTEIN

4. The mad scientist's name was Victor Rattenstein!

5. The action takes place in Ingolstadt, in Bavaria, which is in Southern Germany!"

The studio went totally quiet.

The drumming stopped.

TORTURETAIL looked up at the director. The director frowned and shrugged. TORTURETAIL turned back to the audience.

"The answer to the final question is ... CORRECT!" TORTURETAIL choked on the last word.

The audience cheered. The jury jeered. Shif T. Paws raced up to me and gave me a hug. "You won a million pounds, Stilton!" he cried.

I was so relieved. I felt like a puddle of nacho cheese sauce that has melted in the hot sun.

My tail was safe and so was The Rodent's Gazette!

Shif T. Paws gave me a hug.

THE MYSTERIOUS RAT IS ...

The two stocky rats let me out of the trap. **TORTURETAIL** reluctantly pushed in a wheelbarrow filled with gold coins. Shif T. Paws happily took the wheelbarrow from him.

"When you get right down to it, being on **THE MOUSETRAP** was a big success!" he cried.

An armoured truck took us back to 85 Curds Court. The morning sun was just rising, but a crowd of reporters had gathered at the door. They began shouting questions.

"Mr. Stilton, are you happy you saved your tail?"

"Tell us, were you nervous?"

"Mr. Stilton, would you do it again?"

I did a victory lap through the crowd. "Not for a million pounds of cheddar!" I squeaked.

Shif T. Paws and I went inside the bakery, slamming the door behind us. Bagel Buckwheat approached us, carrying a large cheese pizza. He had written a message in anchovies:

Well done, Stilton!

I was touched. "Thank you, Bagel," I said. "You are a true friend."

Thea ran up, waving a piece of paper. "I've discovered the identity of the mysterious one-eyed rat," she announced. "It's—"

"**WHO IS IT?**" I squeaked.

"What is his name?" Shif T. asked.

"Tell us! Tell us!" shouted the staff.

Thea smiled. "The mysterious one-eyed rat is named FLUSHER POTTYPAWS," she said. "Until three days ago, he owned a company that made sanitary fittings."

"Sanitary fittings?" Mousella repeated. She looked puzzled.

"That's toilets to you and me," said Thea, grinning.

"That figures!" Shif T. Paws said.

"POTTYPAWS started his company thirty years ago," Thea continued. "He is very, very rich. He invented a one-of-a-kind toilet with a warmed-up seat."

"That's right!" I shouted. "I've seen the ads for POTTYPAWS toilets."

I picked up the phone to give him a call. Then I changed my mind. "I want to go talk to him snout-to-snout!" I said.

I left Shif T. Paws to count the gold coins. Then I called a taxi to take me to 17 Swiss Cheese Centre. That used

THE NEW *Westbottom* TOILET
FOR THE MOUSE WITH CLASS!

Button to adjust seat height

Automatic page turner for book lovers

Anti-splash toilet seat cover

Battery-operated flusher

Volume knob for the radio

Silky-smooth toilet paper – embossed with your own initials

Radio that switches on as soon as the seat is lifted

Self-cleaning, antistench toilet brush

Control panels for:
a computer to surf the net from your seat
lighting
privacy blinds

Cheddar sented bathroom deodorant

Toilet seat covered in self-warming synthetic cat fur

to be the address of The Rodent's Gazette. Now it was the home of *The Roaring Rat*.

But not for long, I promised myself.

I had my tail. I had my staff. I had **A MILLION POUNDS**.

That FLUSHER POTTYPAWS had better watch out!

Mr. Flusher
Pottypaws

I rang the doorbell at 17 Swiss Cheese Centre.

"Let me in!" I said forcefully. "My name is Stilton, *Geronimo Stilton*."

The door buzzed open. I stormed down the hallway to my ex-office. Then I pushed open my ex-office door.

A one-eyed rat sat behind the desk. He wore a black patch on his other eye. It made him look like some kind of pirate. He was short and stocky, and his fur was shiny with fur gel. He wore a striped suit and

FLUSHER POTTYPAWS

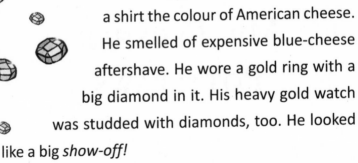

a shirt the colour of American cheese. He smelled of expensive blue-cheese aftershave. He wore a gold ring with a big diamond in it. His heavy gold watch was studded with diamonds, too. He looked like a big *show-off!*

FLUSHER POTTYPAWS growled at me. "By the stench of a thousand toilet brushes! What do you want?"

POTTYPAWS tried to look threatening, but he didn't scare me. I had survived **THE MOUSETRAP**, after all!

"My name is Stilton, *Geronimo Stilton*," I said proudly. "I run The Rodent's Gazette!"

"Trumpeting toilets!" he roared. "What are you doing here? This is no longer your office!"

I laughed. "I just won a million pounds. Now I, too, am very, very rich. You can't use your money to ruin my business anymore!"

POTTYPAWS glared at me. He looked like a tough rat. But I can be tough, too! I kept going.

"This town is too small for the both of us, POTTYPAWS," I said. "The fight is even now!"

POTTYPAWS turned pale. He suddenly looked sad.

"No," he said.

"No, what?" I asked.

He shook his head. "This fight is not even," he said glumly.

I was puzzled. I was expecting more of a fight from this rat. "Why not?" I asked.

POTTYPAWS did not answer for a while. Then he rested his head on the desk and burst into tears.

FLUSHER POTTYPAWS

"This fight will never be even because you are clever, and I don't have what it takes to run a publishing house!"

POTTYPAWS sobbed and sobbed. He practically cried a river of tears. I couldn't help it. I started to feel sorry for him!

SIGNED TOILET PAPER

POTTYPAWS kept sobbing. "I never went to college," he said. "I'm a self-made mouse. I wanted to have a publishing company. I thought all you had to do was pay for it. But I was wrong."

I walked up to him and put a paw on his shoulder. "Cheer up," I said. "You do have a newspaper. *The Roaring Rat*!"

POTTYPAWS opened a drawer in his desk. He took out some papers filled with numbers.

"Take a look at this!" he said. "The newsagents are returning all of my newspapers. The bookstores are returning all of my books. The readers only want The Rodent's Gazette and Stilton Publishing!"

POTTYPAWS began to sob again. I looked at the list of books put out by The Roaring Rat Group. I understood why the public didn't like them. The titles were horrible!

I took pity on poor POTTYPAWS. "It's not your fault you didn't succeed," I told him. "You can't become a publisher overnight. It took me twenty years to learn the business. I was only thirteen when my grandfather began taking me to book fairs."

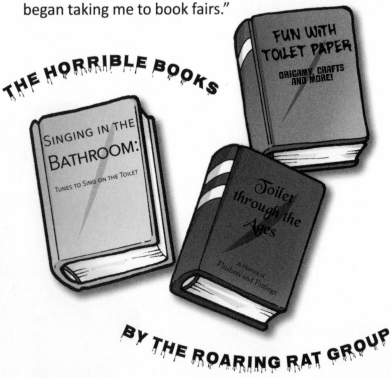

THE HORRIBLE BOOKS

FUN WITH TOILET PAPER
ORIGAMI, CRAFTS AND MORE!

SINGING IN THE BATHROOM:
TUNES TO SING ON THE TOILET

Toilet through the Ages
A History of Flushers and Fittings

BY THE ROARING RAT GROUP

POTTYPAWS blew his snout into a big red pawkerchief with yellow dots. "You're just saying that to cheer me up," he said. "I'm an ignorant mouse. A loser. A third-rat rodent."

I hate to see a mouse get down on himself.

"Come on, don't cry!" I said. "I'm sure you're a fine mouse!"

"Easy for you to say," POTTYPAWS grumbled. "Everyone on Mouse Island knows you. Your books are great. I've read every single one of them."

He reached into his drawer again and took out one of my books: *Four Mice Deep in the Jungle*.

"Would you sign it for me?" he asked.

I thought about the perfect thing to write. Then I signed it:

To my new friend, Flusher Pottypaws. May he soon be signing his own books!

POTTYPAWS sighed. "Thank you, Mr. Stilton. But I'm afraid the best I can ever hope for is **to sign a roll of toilet paper!**"

FIRST-RAT ART

POTTYPAWS was so grateful, he offered to give our offices back to us. I called Mousella, who was happy to hear the news.

"That's wonderful, Mr. Stilton!" she said. "I'll tell the others!"

Moments later, I heard a shout. "Watch your whiskers, here comes Shif T. Paws!"

I knew what was coming. But the door flew open before I could move out of the way. **SPLAT!** The door slammed into me once again.

Shif T. Paws burst into the room. His arms were loaded with books. As he put them back on the shelves, he whistled a happy tune: *Ninety-Nine Morsels of Cheese.*

POTTYPAWS watched Shif T. with a sad look on his face. "Just look at all of your books and newspapers," he said. "You are lucky to have such an interesting job. All I ever get to deal with are flushers and toilet seats."

"But you make lots of money doing it!" I pointed out.

He shook his head. "There are things money can't buy, Stilton. Like culture, for example."

Suddenly, I heard cries outside the window. I looked out to see a crowd of rodents. They were all shouting, "We want The Rodent's Gazette! We want The Rodent's Gazette!"

I smiled. "You want the newspaper?" I shouted back. "Then you shall have it! As of tomorrow, everything is back to normal. You will find The Rodent's Gazette on newsstands! You will find Stilton Publishing's books in every bookstore!"

The crowd cheered. "Hurrah for The Rodent's Gazette!"

I turned back to the office and saw POTTYPAWS standing in the corner. He looked like he was going to cry again.

Shif T. Paws must have noticed, too. He ran up to me, his eyes glittering with excitement. "Stilton, I have a **brilliant** idea!" he said. "When you get right down to it, why don't you two open a publishing house together? You can provide your experience, and POTTYPAWS can provide the money. You can put out art books."

POTTYPAWS brightened up. "I love it! And I have a great idea for a name. We can call it **TOILET ART**."

"That's not bad," I said, trying to be nice. "But maybe we should go with a more classic name. Like ... **FIRST-RAT ART**."

"Great!" POTTYPAWS cried. He crushed me in a tight hug. Then he leaned out the window and shouted, "I have a publishing house, too! Me, FLUSHER POTTYPAWS!"

The crowd stared up at him, bewildered.

"It's called **FIRST-RAT ART**!" he continued. "I don't want to brag, but we're talking high culture here!"

The crowd was silent for a moment. Then they all shouted, **"Yes! Hurrah for Flusher Pottypaws! Hurrah for First-Rat Art!"**

MAKE A NOTE OF THAT, SCRIBBLESCRATCH!

The next morning, I saw a new sign on the door of 17 Swiss Cheese Centre:

FIRST-RAT ART
SERIOUS ARTY-SMARTY ART BOOKS!

POTTYPAWS was already settled in his new office, right next to mine. He was giving some notes to his secretary, Scrawland Scribblescratch. He is a grey rodent with a bald head and thick glasses.

"Art! Yes, art!" POTTYPAWS was saying. Scribblescratch was quickly writing down everything POTTYPAWS said. "Art. Yes, art!" the secretary murmured.

Just then, my **GLOBAL CULTURE CONSULTANT** (GCC) walked past the office. He is Mousias van Raten, the uncle of my assistant editor, **Pinky Pick**.

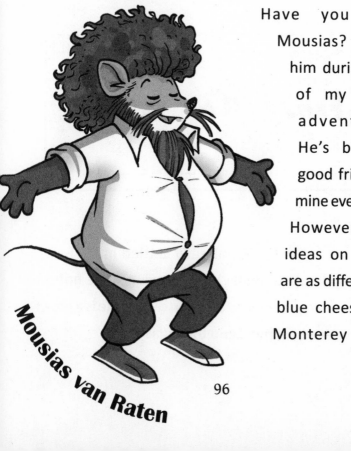

Mousias van Raten

Have you met Mousias? I met him during one of my many adventures. He's been a good friend of mine ever since. However, our ideas on books are as different as blue cheese and Monterey Jack.

96

He thinks every book needs to be Intellectual with a capital 'I'.

Mousias stopped in the doorway. "Excuse me, but I believe that Art should always have a capital 'A'!" he said in a thundering voice.

POTTYPAWS nodded. "Rumbling rest rooms, you're right! Let's fix that, Scribblescratch. Art with a capital 'A'."

Scribblescratch sighed. "Art with a capital 'A'."

Mousias grinned and walked into my office. "**HOLEY CHEESE!** At long last, there is someone in this office who cares about Culture with a capital 'C'. A true intellectual – with a capital 'I'

POTTYPAWS looked as pleased as a shopper who's just found out there's a half-price sale on cheese. "Me? An Intellectual with a capital 'I'? Why not? Let's talk about it."

Pinky Pick

97

Mousias saw his chance. "I have lots of ideas, you know, for some really Artistic, Intellectual books!"

POTTYPAWS waved his paw at me. "Come and listen to this smart rodent's ideas with me, Stilton!"

But I had already slunk off.

RECOLLECTIONS OF
A RAT

Six months later, I heard a car horn outside my home. It was seven o'clock at night.

I looked out the window. A limousine the colour of cheese was parked on the street. A mouse wearing a striped suit was leaning out the window. It was FLUSHER POTTYPAWS, of course!

"Come on down, Stilton, it's late!" he called up. "It's time for the exhibit of **IMPRESSIONABLE** paintings. And after that, there's the **room music** concert!"

I went downstairs and got in the car. "I hope you don't mind me correcting you," I squeaked. "But the paintings are called **IMPRESSIONIST**, not impressionable. And it's **chamber music,** not room music."

POTTYPAWS raised his bushy eyebrows. "**PRANCING PLUNGERS**, I didn't know that!" he thundered. Then he shouted to his secretary in the front seat. "Make a note of that, Scribblescratch!"

"Right away, sir," Scribblescratch said.

POTTYPAWS chuckled and nudged me with his elbow. "At this rate, I'll soon be a truly intellectual mouse," he said. "I'm already writing my autobiography. I think I'll call it *Recollections of a Rat!*"

POTTYPAWS got a dreamy look on his face. "I could print the whole thing on a single roll of toilet paper! That way you can read it one piece at a time, tearing off a piece as you go! We could get a toilet paper company to sponsor us. FLUFFYBOTTOM, maybe. What do you think?"

Before I could answer, he roared at his secretary. **"Make a note of that,** Scribblescratch**!"**

POTTYPAWS turned back to me. "So, what do you think, Partner?"

I didn't want to tell POTTYPAWS what I really thought of his stinky idea. "I'll, uh, think about it," I said. "It certainly is ... **original!**"

Then we reached the exhibit of paintings. We got out of the limousine and went into the art gallery. **FIRST-RAT ART** had organised a party to kick off the exhibition.

POTTYPAWS was thrilled to be there. "I am FLUSHER POTTYPAWS, from the **FIRST-RAT ART** group!" he announced.

He began shaking hands with all of the reporters and art critics. "Hi there! How are you? If I do say so myself, this exhibition **DOESN'T STINK**! Ha, ha, ha."

After a while, he came up to me. "Thank you, Geronimo. I am so happy to be involved in publishing. You have made my wish come true. **YOU ARE A TRUE FRIEND!**"

Maybe POTTYPAWS could become an Intellectual mouse with a capital '**I**' after all!

Just then, I heard a cry. "Watch your whiskers, here comes Shif T. Paws!"

This time, I scurried out of the way as fast as I could. The door opened ... **and missed me!**

"Hey there, Stilton," Shif T. said, shaking my paw. "It's been great working with you."

"It's nice to work with you too, Shif T.," I said, smiling.

I really meant it. **Everything had turned out fine ... thanks to Shif T. Paws!**

ABOUT THE AUTHOR

Born in New Mouse City, Mouse Island, GERONIMO STILTON is Rattus Emeritus of Mousomorphic Literature and of Neo-Ratonic Comparative Philosophy. For the past twenty years, he has been running The Rodent's Gazette, New Mouse City's most widely read daily newspaper.

Stilton was awarded the Ratitzer Prize for his scoops on *The Curse of the Cheese Pyramid* and *The Search for Sunken Treasure*. He has also received the Andersen Prize

for Personality of the Year. His works have been published all over the globe.

In his spare time, Mr. Stilton collects antique cheese rinds and plays golf. But what he most enjoys is telling stories to his nephew Benjamin.

The Rodent's Gazette

1. Main entrance
2. Printing presses (where everything is printed)
3. Accounts department
4. Editorial room (where editors, illustrators, and designers work)
5. Geronimo Stilton's office
6. Geronimo's botanical garden

MAP OF NEW MOUSE CITY

1. Industrial Zone
2. Cheese Factories
3. Angorat International Airport
4. WRAT Radio and Television Station
5. Cheese Market
6. Fish Market
7. Town Hall
8. Snotnose Castle
9. The Seven Hills of Mouse Island
10. Mouse Central Station
11. Trade Centre
12. Movie Theatre
13. Gym
14. Catnegie Hall
15. Singing Stone Plaza
16. The Gouda Theatre
17. Grand Hotel
18. Mouse General Hospital
19. Botanical Gardens
20. Cheap Junk for Less (Trap's store)
21. Parking Lot
22. Mouseum of Modern Art
23. University and Library
24. The Daily Rat
25. The Rodent's Gazette
26. Trap's House
27. Fashion District
28. The Mouse House Restaurant
29. Environmental Protection Centre
30. Harbour Office
31. Mousidon Square Garden
32. Golf Course
33. Swimming Pool
34. Blushing Meadow Tennis Courts
35. Curlyfur Island Amusement Park
36. Geronimo's House
37. Historic District
38. Public Library
39. Shipyard
40. Thea's House
41. New Mouse Harbour
42. Luna Lighthouse
43. The Statue of Liberty
44. Hercule Poirat's Office
45. Petunia Pretty Paws's House
46. Grandfather William's House

MAP OF MOUSE ISLAND

1. Big Ice Lake
2. Frozen Fur Peak
3. Slipperyslopes Glacier
4. Coldcreeps Peak
5. Ratzikistan
6. Transratania
7. Mount Vamp
8. Roastedrat Volcano
9. Brimstone Lake
10. Poopedcat Pass
11. Stinko Peak
12. Dark Forest
13. Vain Vampires Valley
14. Goosebumps Gorge
15. The Shadow Line Pass
16. Penny-Pincher Castle
17. Nature Reserve Park
18. Las Ratayas Marinas
19. Fossil Forest
20. Lake Lake
21. Lake Lakelake
22. Lake Lakelakelake
23. Cheddar Crag
24. Cannycat Castle
25. Valley of the Giant Sequoia
26. Cheddar Springs
27. Sulphurous Swamp
28. Old Reliable Geyser
29. Vole Vale
30. Ravingrat Ravine
31. Gnat Marshes
32. Munster Highlands
33. Mousehara Desert
34. Oasis of the Sweaty Camel
35. Cabbagehead Hill
36. Rattytrap Jungle
37. Rio Mosquito
38. Mousefort Beach
39. San Mouscisco
40. Swissville
41. Cheddarton
42. Mouseport
43. New Mouse City
44. Pirate Ship of Cats

HAVE YOU READ ALL OF GERONIMO'S ADVENTURES?

☐ *Lost Treasure of the Emerald Eye*

☐ *The Curse of the Cheese Pyramid*

☐ *Cat and Mouse in a Haunted House*

☐ *I'm Too Fond of My Fur!*

☐ *Four Mice Deep in the Jungle*

☐ *Paws Off, Cheddarface!*

☐ *Fangs and Feasts in Transratania*

☐ *Attack of the Pirate Cats*

HAPPY READING!